The Adventures of
IJAPA
the Tortoise

Told by Paula B. Sofowora

amlap
publishing

For Femi and Seun

First published in Great Britain in 2012
by Amlap Publishing
P O Box 6144
Basildon
SS14 OWX
www.amlappublishing.com

Acknowledgements
My dearest friends Janet Sherlock and Doreen Nwanko;
teachers Patricia Carpenter and Stephanie Machin;
editor Ruth Nason; illustrator Lisa Parsons; graphic designers
Mark Graves and Simon Berry; Ben Foat, Kate Brightmore,
Cath Bruzzone and Sam Hutchinson and librarian Wendy Levingstone.

ISBN   978 0 9546116 3 7
Printed in Singapore

amlap publishing

Contents

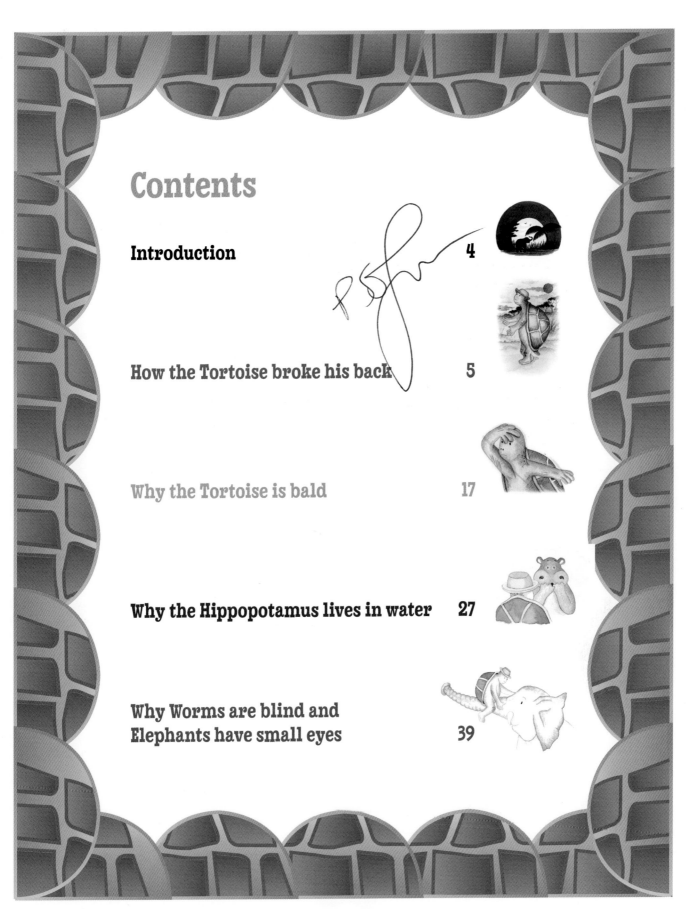

Introduction   4

How the Tortoise broke his back   5

Why the Tortoise is bald   17

Why the Hippopotamus lives in water   27

Why Worms are blind and Elephants have small eyes   39

Introduction

Many West African folk stories are about the Animal Kingdom. Here animals had the same characteristics as people, and animals and people were friends. Often the stories were told by moonlight in the village square or compound. The stories were told to entertain people and to help them understand the right ways to behave. Each story has a moral, which is a message or lesson you can learn from it.

How the Tortoise broke his back

Long ago, all the animals were friends. They walked on two legs, talked, ate and behaved just like people do today.

Ijapa, the tortoise, was known as one of the cleverest of all the animals because of his quick and cunning ways of thinking.

This is the story of how Ijapa broke his back and why, to this day, you can still see the pattern left on his shell.

Every year, the birds held a meeting in the sky. Every year, this meeting was followed with a **BIG FEAST.** Everybody wanted to be invited.

One year, Ijapa received an invitation to be the special guest at the birds' meeting in the sky.

Invitation

We have great pleasure in inviting Ijapa to be the special Guest at this year's meeting in the sky.

Oriole

One of the elders, called Oriole, had chosen Ijapa to be the special guest. Oriole knew of Ijapa's reputation for being quick-thinking and clever.

Who signed?

Birds of all shapes and Sizes and colours
gave a few feathers each, to make Ijapa
his very own pair of wings.
The birds wanted their special guest to
look like them and fly like them on the day
of the meeting in the sky.

Here's the guide who led Ijapa to the meeting.

Everything went according to plan. Ijapa's wings were beautiful. Ijapa could not stop looking in the mirror and preening himself.

Ijapa's wife, Yanibo, and all the other animals said that Ijapa looked very grand indeed. They secretly wished that they had received an invitation and a pair of beautiful wings too.

On the day of the meeting in the sky, all the animals were **DAZZLED** by the brilliant colours of Ijapa's wings. They looked like a **rainbow**.

There was the sound of sweet melody as the birds flapped their wings and called out to each other on their way to the meeting.

Ijapa had his very own guide for the journey. It was exciting for Ijapa to fly.

At the meeting in the sky, Ijapa made a speech to all the birds.

Everyone listened to him eagerly. Some whispered to one another about how wise Ijapa was and how lucky they were that Ijapa was their special guest.

In his speech, Ijapa told everyone to choose a nickname. It sounded a good idea and so all the birds chose nicknames for themselves. The nickname that Ijapa chose for himself was **"EVERYONE"**.

The meeting was going well. Sweet cooking smells floated into the room and Ijapa and all the other guests started to feel hungry. They fidgeted as the waiters brought in steaming dishes of delicious food.

"This is for everyone."

As the waiters laid a dish on the table, they said,

Parrot and Swallow were about to help themselves when Ijapa pointed out that the dish was actually for him – for Everyone. Then, to the surprise of all the birds, Ijapa greedily gobbled it up.

The waiters came in with more delicious food and each time they said,

"This is for everyone."

Ijapa remembered his manners and repeatedly said "Thank you", before tucking in to the dish. Oriole and the hungry birds looked on, upset and annoyed. It was well known that Ijapa was greedy, but nobody had thought about the result of his greediness.

By the time Ijapa had eaten what he wanted, there was ALMOST NOTHING LEFT.

The birds were angry and very hungry. They began to leave, one by one. As they left, they removed the feathers they had given to Ijapa. Ijapa was stranded in the sky.

Ijapa could no longer fly. How could he get home now?

Suddenly Ijapa had a brilliant idea. He saw Cuckoo perched on a tree nearby and said:

"Cuckoo, will you take a message to Yanibo, my wife? Tell her to bring all the soft mattresses, cushions and pillows out of the house and pile them on the ground, so that I will not hurt myself when I jump down from the sky."

Cuckoo said that he would deliver the message to Yanibo.

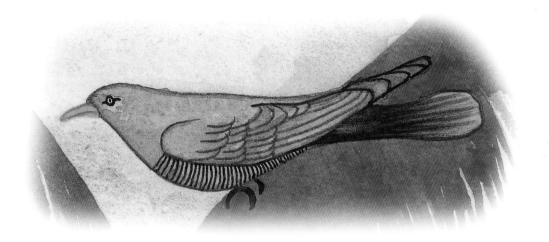

However, Cuckoo knew what Ijapa did at the meeting in the sky. Cuckoo thought that someone should teach Ijapa a lesson, and so he decided **NOT** to give Ijapa's message to Yanibo. Instead, Cuckoo just flew away and never came back.

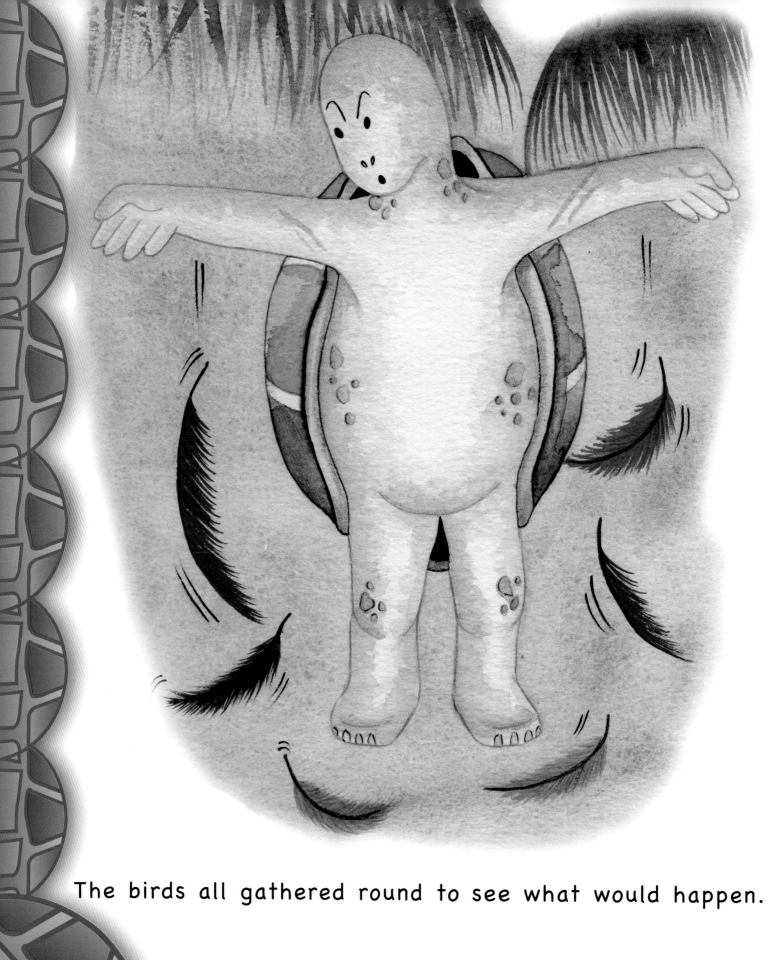

The birds all gathered round to see what would happen.

Ijapa jumped down from the sky. There were no soft mattresses, cushions or pillows and so Ijapa landed on the hard ground. Poor Ijapa

BROKE his shell into lots of little pieces.

Yanibo, Ijapa's wife, had to stick the little pieces together again.

The tortoise still has the same pattern of pieces on his back. Have you noticed it?

Next time you see a tortoise, have a **CLOSER** look.

What is the moral of this story?
The answer is on the next page.

The moral of the story is:

If you play tricks on other people someone is likely to play a trick on you too.

What do you remember?

1. Who is Yanibo?
2. What nickname did Ijapa choose for himself?
3. Can you name three types of birds mentioned in the story?

Can you say what these words mean?

Cunning

Eagerly

Fidgeted

Melody

Repeatedly

Reputation

Speech

Stranded

What did it mean when Ijapa "preened himself" in front of the mirror?

What did it mean when he "tucked into the dish"?

Why the Tortoise is bald

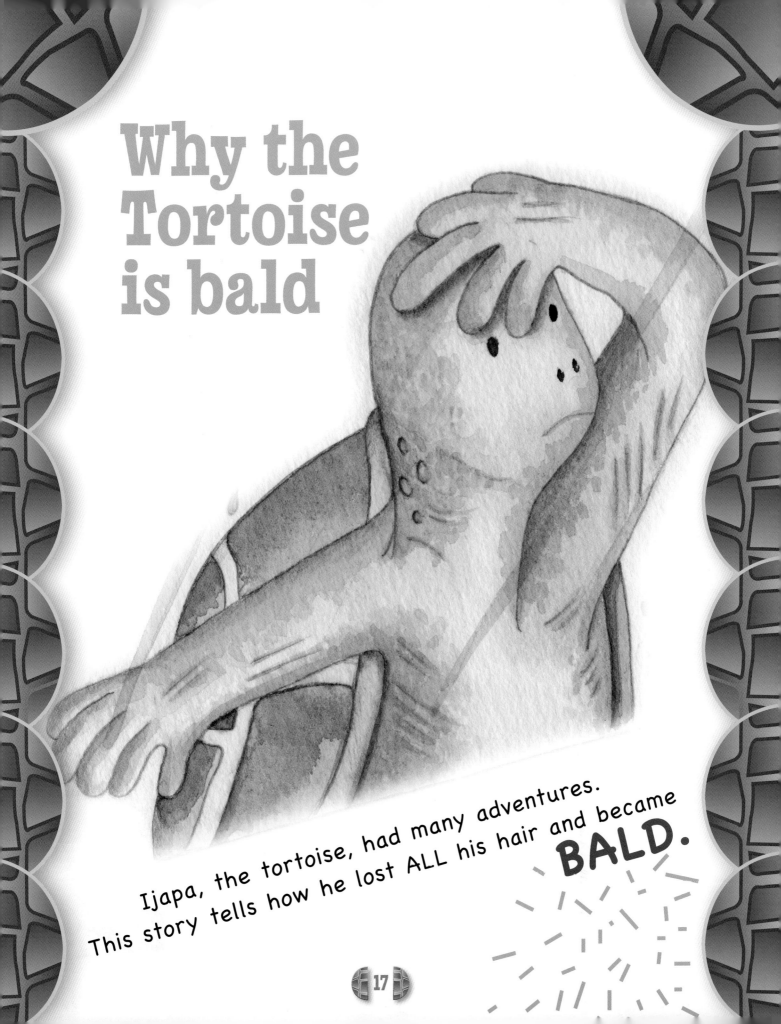

Ijapa, the tortoise, had many adventures. This story tells how he lost ALL his hair and became **BALD.**

It was hot and sunny.
White clouds sailed in the sky, like
FLUFFY BALLS OF COTTON WOOL.

Palm trees swayed
from side to side in
the gentle breeze
and red-necked lizards
sunbathed lazily on
the red-hot sand.

**What colour
is this lizard's
neck?**

Ijapa was sitting on his porch.
He was very pleased because
Yanibo, his girlfriend, had agreed to marry him.

Ijapa was looking forward to meeting Yanibo's
parents, Mama and Baba. He had promised to be
on his best behaviour, because he wanted Mama
and Baba to be proud of him.

It sounded as if the jungle wanted to celebrate the good news with Ijapa. Birds chirped brightly as they flew by. A lion **ROARED** in the distance and a group of monkeys chattered as they played in the **long** green grass. It really was a lovely day, thought Ijapa happily.

Ijapa looked very smart in his new straw hat.

He walked to the house where Yanibo and her parents, Mama and Baba, lived. He knew that Yanibo, his girlfriend, would not be there. She had told him that she would be out with friends.

Ijapa knocked politely. He was a little nervous about meeting Mama and Baba for the first time, on his own.

Mama opened the door with a big smile on her face. She gave Ijapa a great big hug and welcomed him in. Baba was still getting dressed, but he called out a friendly greeting.

Mama knew how much Ijapa loved his food. She had cooked yam porridge, Ijapa's favourite meal.

Ijapa could smell the yam porridge straightaway. He had to stop himself from closing his eyes and licking his lips.

In the dining room a huge bowl of steaming hot yam porridge sat in the middle of the table. Poor Ijapa could not stop himself. While nobody was looking, he tried some. It was **D-E-L-I-C-I-O-U-S** and he gobbled down as much as he could.

There was joy on Ijapa's face, but the joy disappeared when Ijapa heard footsteps coming along the corridor. Quickly, he spooned some porridge into his hat and, without thinking, placed the hat back on his head!

Then Ijapa's polite smile disappeared. Ijapa **wriggled** on his seat. Sweat poured down his face and neck and smoke curled out of his ears. Poor Ijapa could not sit still. He could not wait to get home and remove his hat.

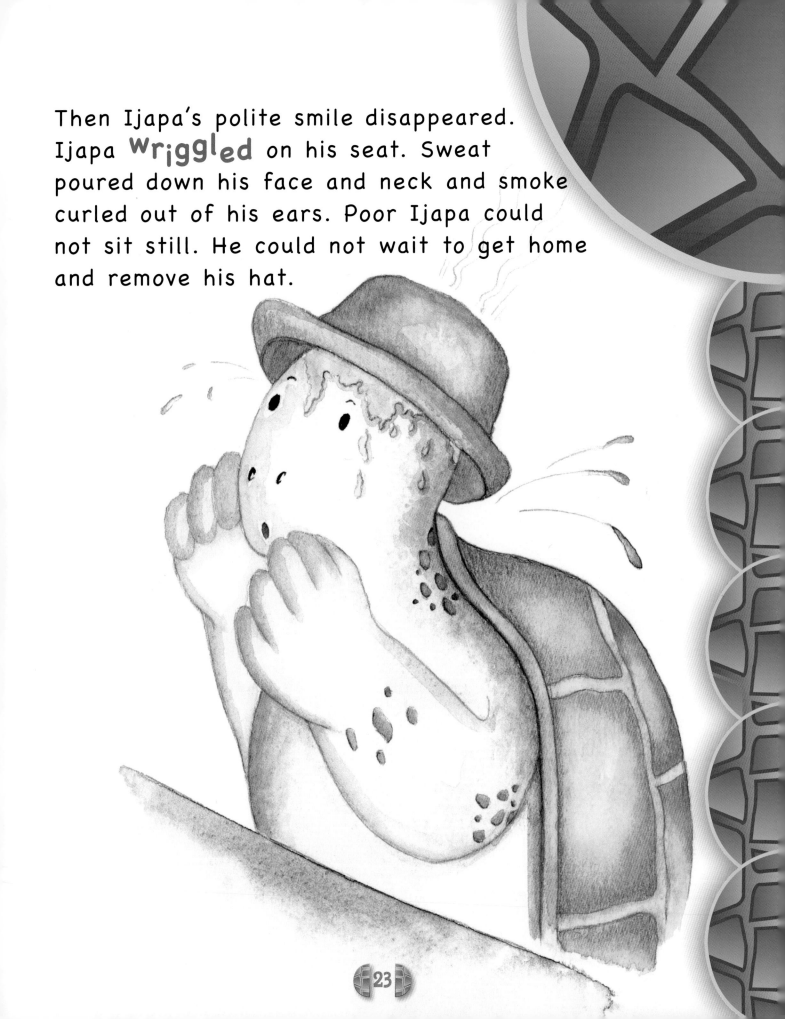

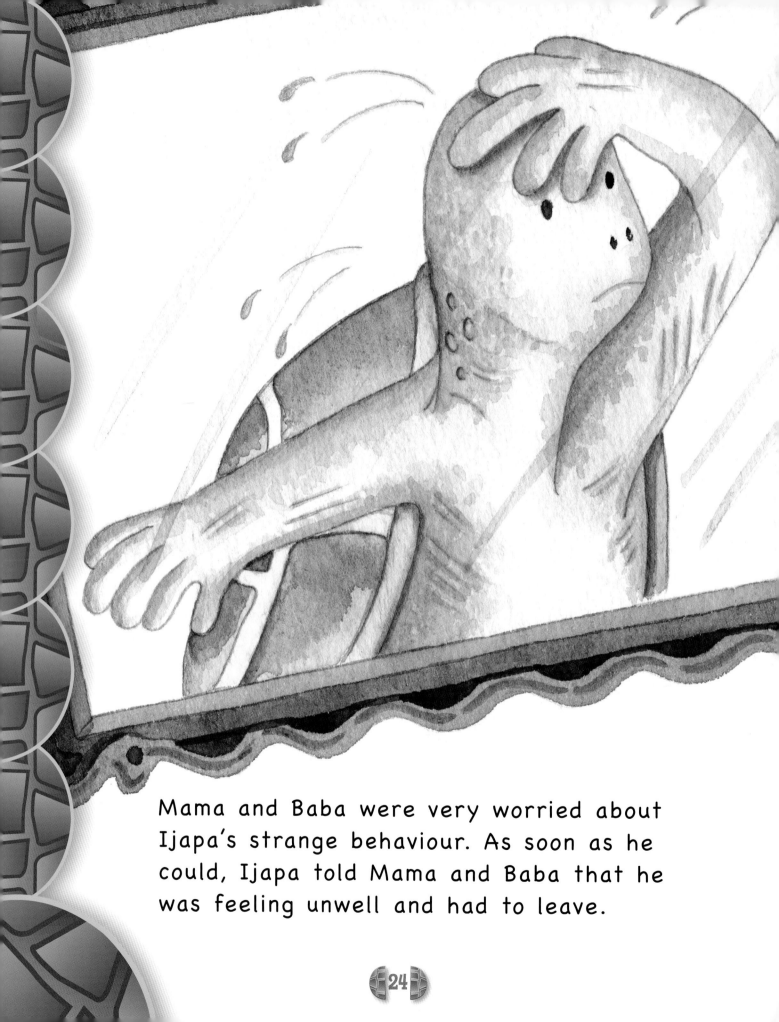

Mama and Baba were very worried about Ijapa's strange behaviour. As soon as he could, Ijapa told Mama and Baba that he was feeling unwell and had to leave.

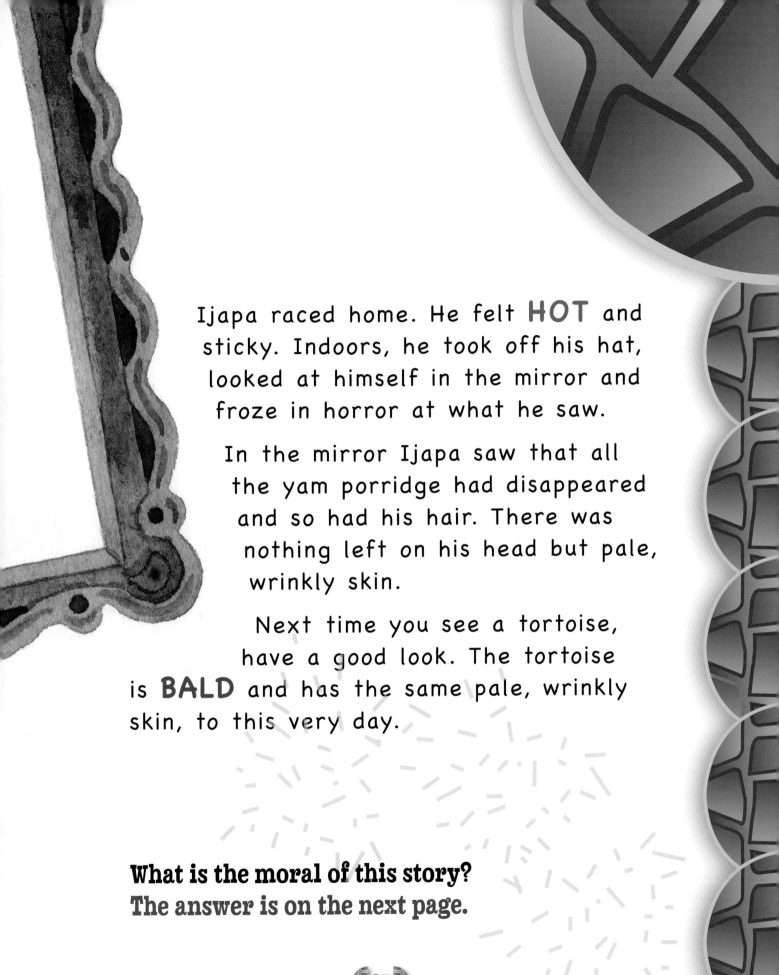

Ijapa raced home. He felt **HOT** and sticky. Indoors, he took off his hat, looked at himself in the mirror and froze in horror at what he saw.

In the mirror Ijapa saw that all the yam porridge had disappeared and so had his hair. There was nothing left on his head but pale, wrinkly skin.

Next time you see a tortoise, have a good look. The tortoise is **BALD** and has the same pale, wrinkly skin, to this very day.

What is the moral of this story?
The answer is on the next page.

The moral of the story is:
Don't be greedy and do not steal.

What do you remember?
1. Who was Ijapa going to visit?
2. What was his favourite food?
3. Which other animals were mentioned in the story?

Can you say what these words mean?
Bald
Celebrate
Delicious
Gobbled
Joy
Nervous
Politely
Porch
Yam

What did it mean when Ijapa had to stop himself from "licking his lips"?

What did it mean when "smoke curled out" of Ijapa's ears?

What did it mean when Ijapa "froze in horror" when he saw himself in the mirror?

What was your favourite part of the story and why?

Why the Hippopotamus lives in water

In this story Ijapa goes to another feast. You will find out that the Hippopotamus lives in water because of something that Ijapa the tortoise did.

In the Animal Kingdom long ago, everyone respected Hippopotamus because of his **large** size. He had seven wives, who were as large as he was. He also had many children, who would grow up to be even larger than their parents.

Every year, Hippopotamus held a feast for all the animals. It was a grand occasion.

GRAND FEAST

Once, just before all the guests sat down to eat, Hippopotamus called for their attention. He stood with his seven very large wives beside him and bellowed,

"Does anyone know my name?"

The animals looked up, puzzled and surprised. For ages everyone had tried to guess what Hippopotamus was called, but nobody knew.

Hippopotamus looked upset, but secretly he was pleased. He said,

"If you do not know my name, you can no longer eat at my table. Perhaps you will have found out my name by the time we all meet again next year."

The animals looked at Hippopotamus in shocked silence. Many had travelled a long way, including Ijapa, the tortoise, who was not at all happy.

Ijapa was not very big, but he loved his food. He had been looking forward to a really good time at the feast. Ijapa was angry that Hippopotamus was turning everyone away.

Ijapa plucked up his courage and asked Hippopotamus,

"What will you do if someone does find out your name?"

Ijapa was already thinking of a plan.

Hippopotamus said, "I will be so ashamed that my family and I will be forced to leave the land and go and live in the water forever."

Hippopotamus did not think that anyone would ever find out his name.

Ijapa was known for his quick and cunning ways of thinking. He knew that Hippopotamus and his family often went to bathe in the river. A few days after the feast-that-never-was, Ijapa waited by the path until the ground shook and a billow of red dust filled the air. These were signs that Hippopotamus, his seven very large wives and all his very large children were coming.

Can you see Ijapa?

Quickly Ijapa curled up inside his shell, by the side of the path. He looked like a stone.

As Hippopotamus, his seven very large wives and all his very large children passed by, Ijapa rolled onto the path. He placed himself so that one of the wives stubbed her toe against his hard shell. She cried out in pain to her husband:

"Oh Isantim, I have hurt my foot. Please can we rest for a while?"

Ijapa had heard what he wanted to hear!

Isantim went to look after his injured wife and Ijapa made his way home, excited and singing happily as soon as no one could hear him.

Ijapa was very pleased, but he would have to wait until Hippopotamus's next feast before he could do anything more.

The next year, just before Hippopotamus's great feast, news had spread to all the animals that Ijapa knew Hippopotamus's name. Ijapa did not tell anyone what he had found out, because he was waiting for his big moment.

The day of the feast arrived. As usual, it was a very grand occasion, but this time there was more excitement in the air. Everyone was wondering whether Ijapa really had found out Hippopotamus's name and, if so, whether Hippopotamus would keep his promise.

Hippopotamus arrived with his seven very large wives and all his very large children. He stood in front of the animals and said there would be no food for any of them unless someone could tell him his name. There was a big **HUSH**.

Ijapa stood up and reminded Hippopotamus: **"You said that if anyone found out your name, you and your family would leave the land and live in the water forever."**

"That's quite right," bellowed Hippopotamus confidently. He was sure that nobody could have found out his name, so he nearly choked with surprise when Ijapa shouted triumphantly:

"Your name is ISANTIM."

All the animals cheered when Hippopotamus agreed that Ijapa had found out his name. Hippopotamus said sorrowfully:

"Let us eat and drink together for the last time. As promised, from this day forward, my family and I will leave the land and live in the river."

This is why, ever since then, Hippopotamuses live mainly in rivers. The only land they come on to is the riverbanks, where they often bask in the sun or catch their prey.

There is a moral to this story. Do you know what it is? The answer is on the next page.

The moral of the story is:

It is not always wise to be over-confident. Think carefully before you make a bold promise.

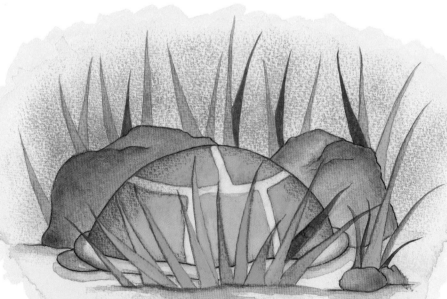

What do you remember?

1. How many wives did Hippopotamus have?
2. How did Ijapa know that Hippopotamus and his family were coming along the path?
3. What made one of Hippopotamus's wives cry out his name?

Can you say what these words mean?

Bask
Bellowed
Billow
Confidently
Injured
Prey
Respected
Sorrowfully
Triumphantly

Why was the feast called "the-feast-that-never-was"?

What did it mean when Ijapa "plucked up his courage"?

Why Worms are blind and Elephants have small eyes

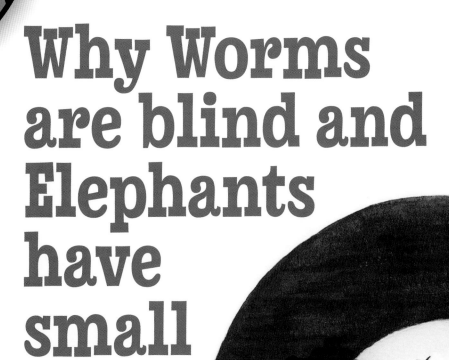

Everyone knew how much Ijapa, the tortoise, loved food. Ijapa ate and ate and never seemed to feel full up, although he was only small.

At the beginning of this story Ijapa is looking forward to another feast, but he is not the only one who loves eating.

The feast takes place near the time of the full moon.

It was full moon and, in a few days, there would be a feast to celebrate the end of the dry season.

Elephant always ate more than anyone else at feasts like this, because of his size. Ijapa thought this wasn't fair and so he decided to teach Elephant a lesson.

Ijapa rubbed his hands together with delight when he thought of his plan. He filled a small bag with dried shrimps and palm kernels. This was a special treat that all the animals liked. Ijapa carried the bag on his way to visit Elephant.

It was a lovely evening and rather nice and cool for a change. Ijapa passed Vulture and Zebra on the way. They appeared to be in a great hurry and did not notice Ijapa in their rush.

What is in Ijapa's bag?

Soon Ijapa came to the river where Elephant was bathing. Ijapa sat down on a large rock and made himself comfortable. Then he called out to Elephant and greeted him. "Are you well, Elephant?"

Elephant looked round in surprise and spotted Ijapa on the rock.

"I am well, my friend," Elephant said, shaking water off his huge, leathery back. Elephant was feeling hungry and wondered what his wife had cooked for them to eat. "What are you doing here?" he asked Ijapa politely.

"I am on my way to see my sick uncle," Ijapa lied, in a sad voice. "I am just stopping for a rest and a bite to eat."

Then Elephant saw that Ijapa appeared to be really enjoying the food he was putting into his mouth.

"What are you eating?" Elephant asked, with interest this time.

"Mmmmmmmm," said Ijapa, shutting his left eye craftily. "You won't believe me. It's my left eye and it's delicious." (He was lying again, knowing that Elephant would want to try some.) "It tastes just like dried shrimp and palm kernels. Do you want a bite?"

"Yes please," said Elephant. He did not stop to think why anyone would eat their eye. He could feel hunger rumbling deep within his massive belly.

"**Mmmmmmmm**, it is really delicious! Have you got any more?" Elephant asked, licking his lips.

"No," said Ijapa, "but why don't you remove **your** left eye and you can have some of your own. I will help you, if you like."

"All right," said Elephant and before
he could change his mind, he lifted Ijapa
up with his trunk. Quick as a flash, Ijapa
gently removed Elephant's left eye
and then let Elephant eat more of
the tasty mixture of dried shrimp
and palm kernels.

Elephant
believed that the
tasty food he was
eating was his own left
eye and he was so greedy for
more that he asked Ijapa to remove his
right eye too. Again, Elephant lifted Ijapa
with his trunk. Again Ijapa quickly removed
Elephant's right eye and then gave him some
of the dried shrimp and palm kernels to eat.

Only when Elephant stopped eating did he realise
that he was now completely blind.

Elephant thrashed around wildly, trumpeting loudly.
Ijapa slid down and scurried away.

"Foolish creature," Ijapa thought to himself.
"That will teach Elephant not to be so greedy!"

Elephant couldn't see where he was going and continued to thrash around, using his trunk to pull up anything that he bumped into. He kept calling out to Ijapa for help, but there was no answer.

Finally Elephant realised that Ijapa had played a nasty trick on him.

Elephant did not like having no eyes and started to think how to get another pair. He decided to play a trick on someone else and soon he thought of a plan. Elephant decided to ask one of the other animals to lend him a pair of eyes for a while, because he had lost his own.

While he was thinking who to ask, Worm crept by and Elephant almost trod on him.

"**Watch out!**" cried Worm in alarm. "You almost squashed me."

"I can't watch out," said Elephant, miserably. "I have lost my eyes. Can you lend me yours for a while, so I can find them?"

Worm was flattered that Elephant was asking him for help. Elephant had never asked Worm for a favour before.

Without thinking any more, Worm removed his eyes and gave them to Elephant. Worm's eyes were very small indeed, but Elephant accepted them quickly, before Worm could change his mind.

Have you noticed that Elephants have very small eyes and that Worms are blind? Next time you see either of them, have a closer look.

There is a moral to this story. Do you know what it is?
The answer is on the next page.

The moral of the story is:
Think before you act and don't be greedy.

What do you remember?
1. When was the feast going to take place?
2. What was the special treat that all the animals liked to eat?
3. What lies did Ijapa tell in the story?

Can you say what these words mean?
Craftily
Dry season
Flattered
Massive
Miserably
Palm kernels
Rumbling
Scurried
Thrash
Trumpeted

What did it mean when Ijapa "rubbed his hands together with delight"?